The HUMBLEBEE HUNTER

Inspired by the Life & Experiments of

Charles Darwin and his *Children*

DEBORAH HOPKINSON *pictures by* JEN CORACE

DISNEY • HYPERION BOOKS

New York

All rights reserved. Published by Disney • Hyperion Books, an imprint of Disney Book Group. No part
of this book may be reproduced or transmitted in any form or by any means, electronic or mechanical,
including photocopying, recording, or by any information storage and retrieval system, without written
permission from the publisher.
For information address Disney • Hyperion Books, 114 Fifth Avenue, New York, New York 10011-5690.
First Edition
10 9 8 7 6 5 4 3 2 1
ILS No. F850-6835-5
288 2009
Printed in Singapore
Set in Cooper Oldstyle
Book design by Teresa Kietlinski Dikun
Reinforced binding
ISBN 978-1-4231-1356-0
Library of Congress Cataloging-in-Publication Data on file.
Visit www.hyperionbooksforchildren.com

For Andy —D.H.

To Debbie —J.C.

One summer afternoon, Mother and Cook
tried to teach me to bake a honey cake.

But raspberries glistened in the sun, and birds
brushed the air with song.

More than anything, I wanted to be *outside*.

Then, out the window, I saw Father, home from
walking on his Thinking Path.

He stopped in the kitchen garden and bent over the
beans. He wanted to study the bees.

Mother smiled and brushed a speck of flour from my cheek.

"Henrietta, I think your father would become a bee, if he could. Just like them, he's always busy."

I smiled back. All of us children knew Father loved nature as well as he loved us.

We liked to poke into the study to see his microscope, and crowd around his feet to hear the stories he told.

"When I was your age," he'd say, "I spent more time with bugs than books. Once I caught two rare beetles, one in each hand, and then I spied a third beetle.

"How could I catch all three?"

I laughed; I knew what happened next.

"You put a beetle in your mouth, Father, but you had to spit it out, and they all got away!"

My favorite stories, though, were about Father roaming the world to collect fossils, shells, sea creatures, and plants.

I imagined myself beside him, touching the back of a giant tortoise, watching iguanas dive, or laughing at a blue-footed booby dance!

Father was still a collector. And most of all he collected questions. We grew up asking *what?* and *why?* and *how?*

When Father studied worms, Lizzie and I stuck knitting needles in the ground to try to measure their holes.

Willy and I helped Father put seeds in salt water, to see if they might still grow if they were carried across the seas.

Horace watched and counted snakes.

George and Lenny gathered moths.

And once, to test if worms could hear, Franky played his bassoon over their heads.

(The worms didn't seem to notice.)

Now I craned my neck and looked outside. What *was* Father doing there among the bees?

"Etty, do pay attention," Mother chided. "You're getting flour everywhere."

All at once Father stood tall in the doorway. I could almost hear his mind buzzing with an idea, a problem, a pattern to figure out—an experiment.

"Etty, bring the flour shaker," he called. My apron flew off, and we all came running.

"What's the *question*?" I asked.

"I am wondering," Father mused, "just how many
flowers a humblebee might visit in a minute."

I clapped my hands.

Bees were chosen! Bees were dusted!
Mine was round and black and gold.
"Shake lots of flour on her, Father," I said, "so I can
see her well."

Father drew out his watch. Our Great Bee Experiment was about to begin.

"Now, when I say 'Start,' count each flower *your* bee visits in one full minute," he called.

"But, Father, what if . . . what if I can't count that high?" cried little Horace.

Father smiled. "Your job, Horace, is to run with Polly on the grass. We don't want a terrier scaring our bees."

I took a breath and kept my bee in sight.
"Hurry, Father, before I lose it."
At last he shouted,
"Ready . . .
start!"

One, two, three . . .

My bee and I, both dusted white, working, working
at our task. I bent my head so close to hers:

Four, five, six . . .

How quick and sure this tiny creature was—she
seemed to know exactly where to go.

Seven,

eight,

nine . . .

If she found a flower dry, she flitted quickly to the next.

Ten,

eleven,

twelve . . .

Her search for nectar never stopped, and while she
darted and she buzzed, her legs spread grains of pollen.
Thirteen,
fourteen . . .
Bee and blossom, blossom and bee!

Lenny giggled, counting loudly.
But my fuzzy bee and I did not look up.

Fifteen,

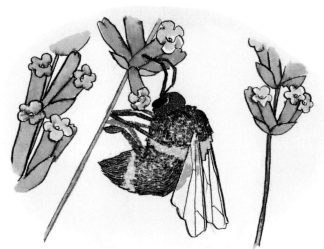 sixteen . . .

I moved closer,
        closer.

Seventeen . . .

Eighteen . . .

Now the lavender is my world too, and I a gentle humblebee, probing just this flower, then the next.

Nineteen, twenty . . .

TWENTY–ONE!

"STOP!"

Charles Darwin

Charles Darwin was born in Shrewsbury, England, on February 12, 1809, the same day as another towering figure in history, Abraham Lincoln. As a young man, Darwin served for five years as naturalist aboard the *H.M.S. Beagle*. Upon his return to London in 1836, Darwin researched his specimens, and worked to develop scientific theories to explain the diversity of life on earth. He concluded that all life on earth evolved, or developed gradually, over millions of years through a process called natural selection.

Darwin's theories were put forth in his book *On the Origin of Species by Means of Natural Selection* (1859), which is usually referred to simply as *The Origin of Species*. Today Darwin is recognized as the father of modern biology.

The Darwin Family

In addition to being a bold thinker and pioneering scientist, Darwin was a devoted husband and father.

Darwin married his cousin Emma Wedgewood in 1839. In 1842, the couple moved to the village of Down, in Kent, England. There, at Down House, Darwin spent the rest of his life until his death in 1882. The Darwins had ten children, seven of whom lived to adulthood: William (1839–1914), Anne (1841–1851), Mary (who died a few weeks after her birth in 1842), Henrietta "Etty" (1843–1929), George (1845–1912), Elizabeth (1847–1926), Francis (1848–1925), Leonard (1850–1943), Horace (1851–1928), and Charles (1856–1858).

Darwin conducted experiments and corresponded with scientists and amateur naturalists throughout his life. He made his study, his gardens, his greenhouse, and his pigeon coop his laboratories. Janet Browne, author of a two-volume biography of Darwin, notes that Emma and the Darwin children often participated in his scientific work—doing experiments in the garden with bees (humblebees are what we call bumblebees), worms, and plants, assisting with correspondence, and proof-reading and helping to edit Darwin's books.

This fictional story is inspired by Darwin's love of nature and children, and what we know of the life of the Darwin family at Down House.

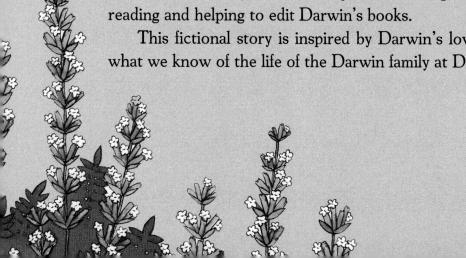

E
Hop   Hopkinson, Deborah.   2787
             The humblebee hunter

DATE   BROD 05/11
          BORROWER'S NAME   16.99

E
Hop   Hopkins

          The
          hun

DUE DA

000 082